Dear Parents and Educators,

Welcome to Penguin Young Readers! As parents and educators, you know that each child develops at his or her own pace—in terms of speech, critical thinking, and, of course, reading. Penguin Young Readers recognizes this fact. As a result, each Penguin Young Readers book is assigned a traditional easy-to-read level (1–4) as well as a Guided Reading Level (A–P). Both of these systems will help you choose the right book for your child. Please refer to the back of each book for specific leveling information. Penguin Young Readers features esteemed authors and illustrators, stories about favorite characters, fascinating nonfiction, and more!

Corduroy Makes a Cake

LEVEL **2**

GUIDED READING LEVEL **I**

This book is perfect for a **Progressing Reader** who:
- can figure out unknown words by using picture and context clues;
- can recognize beginning, middle, and ending sounds;
- can make and confirm predictions about what will happen in the text; and
- can distinguish between fiction and nonfiction.

Here are some **activities** you can do during and after reading this book:
- Word Repetition: Reread the story and count how many times you read the following words: *cake*, *box*, *mess*, *birthday*, *batter*, *picked*. Then, on a separate piece of paper, work with the child to write a new sentence for each word.
- Problem/Solution: The problem in this story is that Corduroy has trouble making a cake for Lisa. How does Corduroy try to solve this problem? What does he give Lisa in the end?

Remember, sharing the love of reading with a child is the best gift you can give!

—Sarah Fabiny, Editorial Director
   Penguin Young Readers program

*Penguin Young Readers are leveled by independent reviewers applying the standards developed by Irene Fountas and Gay Su Pinnell in *Matching Books to Readers: Using Leveled Books in Guided Reading*, Heinemann, 1999.

PENGUIN YOUNG READERS

An Imprint of Penguin Random House LLC

The Library of Congress has catalogued the Viking edition
under the following Control Number: 2001000511

ISBN 9781524788636 (pbk)   10 9 8 7 6 5 4 3 2 1
ISBN 9781524788643 (hc)   10 9 8 7 6 5 4 3 2 1

PENGUIN YOUNG READERS

LEVEL 2
PROGRESSING READER

CORDUROY Makes a Cake

by Alison Inches
illustrated by Allan Eitzen
based on the characters created by Don Freeman

Penguin Young Readers
An Imprint of Penguin Random House

"Today is my birthday,"
Lisa said.

"I'm having a party!"

Lisa gave Corduroy a hug.

Then she left for school.

A birthday party? thought

Corduroy.

I will make Lisa a Corduroy Cake!

Corduroy got everything

he needed:

1 cake mix

2 cake pans

2 cans of pink frosting

1 bowl

2 eggs

1 cup of water

And one thing he did not need.

Crash!

A bag of flour.

Corduroy brushed himself off.

Then, *r-r-r-rip!*

He poured the cake mix

into the bowl.

Crack! Plop! Splash!

He added the eggs and water.

Then he turned on the mixer.

WHIRRRR!

The batter hit the walls.

It hit the floor.

It hit Corduroy.

"This is fun!" said Corduroy.

Then he put the batter

into the pans.

But there was not enough batter.

"Oh dear," said Corduroy.

"I need more cake mix."

He looked high and low.

But there was no more cake mix.

Then he saw a box

on the counter.

He opened it.

"A cake!" said Corduroy.

"Now I don't need to make one."

But the cake had nothing on it.

"It needs words," said Corduroy.

He put the pink frosting

into a bag.

"I can write on it," he said.

"But first I need practice."

He took the frosting

to the bathroom.

He wrote on the tub.

He even wrote on the mirror.

"Wow!" said Corduroy.

"Now I am good!"

Then, *Click!*

He heard a key in the door.

"Somebody's coming!"

said Corduroy.

Bear Hugs

He ran into the sewing

room and hid under a shelf.

Clunk!

A box fell on his head.

Then he heard a voice

in the kitchen.

"What a mess!" cried the voice.

Lisa's mother! thought Corduroy.

He listened to her feet.

Click, click, click.

They walked one way.

Click, click, click.

They walked the other way.

Sweep! Bang! Clank!

The feet ran upstairs

and into the bathroom.

He heard a shout.

The feet ran downstairs.

Corduroy came out from under

the boxes.

He felt terrible.

He had not made a cake for Lisa.

He had just made a mess.

But then Corduroy had an idea.

He picked up a pink button.

Neat!

And a green button.

Cool!

And another!

And another!

Corduroy got to work.

Soon he forgot about the cake
and the mess.

He even forgot he felt terrible

until . . .

Click! Click! Click!

Lisa's mother!

Corduroy hid inside the box.

Creak!

The door opened.

"What's this?"

said her mother.

"It must be

for Lisa!"

23

She picked up the box with
Corduroy and put it on a table.

Corduroy heard things

from inside the box.

He heard the doorbell.

Ding! Dong!

He heard children's voices.

He heard laughter and horns.

25

Then he heard

a voice say,

"Where's Corduroy?"

It was Lisa.

"Corduroy will turn up,"

said her mother.

"It's time for presents."

"Yes!" cried her friends.

Lisa opened a big present.

"A tea set!" she said.

Lisa opened a little present.

"A necklace!" she said.

Then she picked up the box

with Corduroy.

"This box looks like a cake!"

said Lisa.

She shook the box.

Corduroy went up and down.

She shook it again.

Corduroy went from side to side.

Then Lisa took off the lid

and looked inside.

"Corduroy!" she cried.

Lisa picked Corduroy up.

"I love my Corduroy Cake!"

said Lisa.

Corduroy felt very proud.

Happy birthday, Lisa! he thought.

"Happy birthday!"
said her friends.

Then they shouted,

"Hooray for Lisa!

Hooray for Corduroy!"

And hooray for my Corduroy Cake!

thought Corduroy.